Love, Coco

Cute
as a
Button

WOOF!

Cute as a Button

Wendy Loggia

A Skylark Book
New York · Toronto · London · Sydney · Auckland

RL: 3.5, AGES 007–010

CUTE AS A BUTTON

A Bantam Skylark Book / March 2001

ISBN: 0-553-48734-5

Visit us on the Web! www.randomhouse.com/kids

**Educators and librarians, for a variety of teaching tools, visit us at
www.randomhouse.com/teachers**

Published simultaneously in the United States and Canada

BANTAM SKYLARK is an imprint of Random House Children's Books, a division of
Random House, Inc. SKYLARK BOOK and colophon and BANTAM BOOKS and
colophon are registered trademarks of Random House, Inc. Bantam Books,
1540 Broadway, New York, New York 10036.

PRINTED IN THE UNITED STATES OF AMERICA

OPM   10 9 8 7 6 5 4 3 2 1

To Françoise Bui.
You're the cat's meow.

Chapter One

"Ooh, kissy, kissy, kissy," Lauren cooed, touching Coco's round black nose to hers. Then she kissed her puppy's muzzle, giggling as the soft hairs tickled her lips. "I love you so much!"

"Let me see her," Emily Conner begged, inching closer.

"She's so little!" Kaia Hopkins said, reaching to pet Coco's puffy white hair.

"And light!" Lauren said, lifting the bichon frise high above their heads. She giggled again. Having Coco made her want to smile all the time!

Everything had happened so quickly. One day she didn't have a dog—and the next day she did!

Ever since she'd seen Toto hop into Dorothy's basket in *The Wizard of Oz*, Lauren Parker had wanted a dog. Her dad had wanted a dog too. Even her mom had agreed that a pooch might be fun. The problem was that Dad said it was up to Lauren and her mom to pick out the kind of dog they would get.

Lauren was not a very good decision maker. Neither was her mom. They couldn't decide! Big or small? Black or white? Finally they came up with four requirements.

To be a member of the Parker family,
our dog must be:

Cute!
Fluffy!
Small!
And it should not shed.

Then, bingo! A friend of Lauren's mom had a female bichon frise. Her bichon frise had puppies. They were twelve weeks old. The friend called Lauren's mom and asked if they would like one.

"What is it called again?" Lauren had asked when her mom had told her.

"A bichon frise," Mommy had repeated. It sounded like *bee-SHAWN free-ZAY*, and Lauren wasn't too sure about it. She had imagined herself with something ordinary, like a poodle. Or a Westie. Then she saw a picture of a bichon frise. Bichons frises were adorable!

Did she want one?

Do dogs bark?

"I'm so glad you guys could come over," Lauren said, leaning against the trunk at the foot of her bed and holding Coco tight. "I've had her since Friday and it's already Sunday! I couldn't wait for you to meet her!"

"Wild schnauzers couldn't keep me away!"

Kaia said. "Hi, Coco Puff." She nuzzled the puppy's head. Coco sniffed Kaia's black curls. "I love her name."

"Me too. It's just like hot chocolate!" Emily smiled, revealing the tiny gap between her two front teeth. "I wish Lucky was here to play with her."

Lucky was Emily's new yellow Labrador retriever puppy. She was still too little to meet new dogs.

"I do too," Lauren said. Lucky was really cute. "But Coco spells her name *C-O-C-O*, not *C-O-C-O-A*. See?" She lifted the gold-colored ID tag from the dog's collar. "There's no *A* on the end."

"Oh! I thought you named her that because you love hot cocoa," Emily said, her brown eyes puzzled.

"Uh-uh. She's named after Coco Chanel," Lauren explained.

"Is she a famous model?" Kaia asked, striking a pose.

Lauren shook her head. "Close. She was a famous French clothing designer." Lauren's grandmother, Miss Marie, had told Lauren all about Coco Chanel. "*Bichon* is French for 'lapdog.'"

"Maybe if I get a dog, I'll name him Cupcake, after the famous American dessert," Kaia said, patting her T-shirt–covered tummy.

"If you do that, we'll have Lucky Coco Cupcake," Emily told her.

They all giggled.

Coco began to squirm. "Put her down," Emily urged, patting the floor beside her. "She looks like she wants to be free."

Lauren chewed on her lip. Coco had never been in Lauren's bedroom before, and Lauren didn't want her to have an accident. Mommy had made an Exception tonight; normally the puppy had to stay downstairs. But this was a special occasion, Lauren decided. This was the first time Coco was meeting Lauren's very best friends!

"Okeydokey," Lauren said, gently placing her puppy on the pale lilac-colored carpet.

Coco stopped. She looked at the girls. And then she was off.

"She's under the desk!" Emily squealed.

"By the bookshelf!" Kaia cried.

A little white cloud of hair popped up behind Lauren's wicker laundry hamper. "Coco!" Lauren clapped. "Come here, Coco. Come here, good girl!"

Coco tilted her head. Her round dark eyes twinkled. A sliver of pink tongue darted in and out.

She bolted.

"She's like a tornado!" Emily said as Coco ran in circles around Lauren's bedroom. Faster. And faster. And faster!

"Wheeeee!" Kaia said, getting up and spinning in her own circle, her arms outstretched.

"My head's spinning too," Emily said, falling backward where she sat on the floor.

That made Coco run even faster!

Lauren couldn't believe Coco's small legs could move so quickly. She'd never seen Coco like this! She was crazy!

Coco disappeared under Lauren's bed. The bedspread fluttered in her wake. The girls waited expectantly.

"What's she doing?" Kaia wondered aloud, dropping dizzily to the ground.

"She's playing hide-and-seek!" Lauren said gleefully, pushing back her long blond hair.

Emily crawled over to the bed. "I don't think so," she said, lifting up the dust ruffle. Coco was chewing on Lauren's bedpost!

"No, no, Coco!" Lauren cried, pulling her away. She could feel the puppy's thumping heartbeat.

"Check out the teeth marks." Kaia pointed to the bed. Sure enough, the white wood was dented with little grooves. It was wet, too. "Doggie slobber!" Kaia shouted.

"Puppy teeth are so sharp," Emily said.

"Just what I need. My mom would be so mad if she found out," Lauren said worriedly. Coco licked her face. "You mischief maker, you!" Lauren told her. Before the puppy could wriggle free, there was something Lauren wanted to show her friends. She handed Coco over to Emily. "Hold her just a sec."

Lauren ran over to her toy chest. On top was a small plaid suitcase. Lauren undid the buckle and unzipped it. Inside were four small doggie sweaters and a zippered case full of hair bows.

"Look at what my mom ordered from Pet Parade," Lauren said, taking out a tiny hand-made pink-and-blue sweater and a matching hair bow. She couldn't decide which one she liked better.

"I love it!" Emily said, touching it.

"Let's play dress-up," Kaia suggested.

"I tried to put a sweater on Coco before," Lauren admitted. "She was too wiggly."

"Why don't I hold her while you guys do the sweater?" Emily offered.

Coco wiggled. Lauren struggled. Kaia tugged.

"You almost had it!" Emily cried as Coco's head popped out from under Kaia's arm.

Kaia waved the sweater in the air. "What a squirmer!"

"I don't want to hurt her, you guys," Lauren said anxiously as Coco watched them. "Her body's so little."

Coco could tell something was up. And she didn't want any part of it. Before they could try again, she raced for the door.

"Wait, Coco," Kaia called, picking up the pink-and-blue ribbon. "You forgot your bow!"

Chapter Two

"**M**ommy!" Lauren yelled toward her open doorway. "We lost Coco!"

"I found her," came her mom's voice a few seconds later.

Phew! Lauren collapsed backward on the carpeted floor. Her room sure was awfully quiet without Coco tearing up the place.

"She's really cute, Lauren," Kaia said, flopping across Lauren's canopied bed.

Emily was busy looking at some stuff on Lauren's desk. "What's this?" she asked, holding up a sheet of gold paper.

"Ooh, with all the excitement I almost forgot to tell you," Lauren said. "I'm going to enter Lakeville's first annual Little Miss Maple Contest. That paper explains the rules."

"What's the Little Miss Maple Contest?" Emily asked. "Do you have to climb a tree?"

Lauren giggled. Emily loved doing outdoorsy things like that. "No. Haven't you guys heard? It's a contest to celebrate Lakeville." That was the city where they lived. "The girl who wins Little Miss Maple gets a trophy and has her picture in the paper and everything."

Lauren's mom owned a flower shop in town. Someone from the mayor's office had come around to all the stores and passed out flyers about the contest. That was how Lauren had found out about it. It was sponsored by some of Lakeville's shopkeepers. Lauren's mom had chosen not to be a sponsor so that Lauren would be eligible.

"You'll be famous!" Kaia said, batting her eyelashes.

"Do you think so?" Lauren asked. She hadn't thought about that.

Emily pointed to Lauren's special shelf. "I bet you'll get another trophy to put up there," she said. There were trophies for tap dancing. Gymnastics. Even one for a bracelet Lauren had made out of seashells that won the Kraftie Kids competition at summer camp the year before.

Lauren liked to compete. It was fun! But she still got butterflies every time. Sometimes they were little butterflies. Moths, she and her mom called them. And sometimes they were big butterflies. Those were monarchs.

"So what do you have to do?" Kaia asked.

Lauren chewed her bottom lip. "Well, I have to wear a maple-leaf-themed outfit," she said, trying to remember what her mom had told her. "And I can have accessories—but they need to relate somehow to maple leaves."

"Maybe you can carry a bottle of maple syrup," Emily suggested. "Maple syrup comes from maple trees."

Kaia scrunched up her nose. "I think Lauren would get kind of sticky."

Lauren nodded. "I think so too."

"You could take a picture of our school with you," Kaia pointed out.

That was true. They all were in Mrs. Williams's third-grade class at Curly Maple Elementary.

Emily studied the gold sheet of paper for a moment. " 'Little Miss Maplettes may have the following accessories: baskets, umbrellas, hats, and pets,' " she read aloud.

"Pets!" Kaia clapped her hands. "Coco would be the perfect accessory!"

"Yeah!" Emily said, tossing the paper in the air.

Lauren scratched her head. *Coco? In the Little Miss Maple Contest?* She let her breath out with a whoosh. "I don't know about that. Don't you think all the noise might be too much for her? She's only three months old," she reminded them.

"Puppies need to meet other people and animals," Emily told her. "This would be the perfect opportunity!"

Lauren considered the idea. Emily knew everything there was to know about dogs. If she thought being in the contest would be good for Coco, it probably would be.

"But do you think Coco would do okay?" Lauren asked. She had done this type of thing before . . . but Coco hadn't. What if Coco went wild at the contest, just the way she had in Lauren's bedroom? What if she chewed on a judge's leg? Or worse?

"Okay? She'd help you win!" Kaia declared.

Just then Lauren remembered. "Ooh, I almost forgot. Look at what we got Coco at the mall." She went back to the little plaid suitcase and pulled out a tan sweater. Little brown-and-green leaves were knitted into the pattern. She held it up so Emily and Kaia could see it too.

Kaia's eyes widened. "Coco will be a real cutie patootie in that."

"It's almost like fate made you buy that sweater," Emily said excitedly. "It's perfect."

Lauren looked at her friends' faces. She looked back at the sweater. And she looked at the Polaroid of Coco she had put in her Popsicle-stick frame next to her white wooden lampstand, the one with the base that spelled out DREAM.

Whenever Lauren wasn't sure about something, she looked at that lamp. Seeing DREAM always made her want to try to do big things. New things. Things other people only dreamed of doing.

"Okay!" she said. "I'll do it! If my mom says it's okay, I'll enter the Little Miss Maple Contest with Coco!"

Winning was always fun . . . but winning with Coco by her side—or in her basket—would be twice as special!

Chapter Three

"Look! A new girl!" Emily whispered to Lauren as they hung their jackets on their hooks in room 302.

A girl Lauren had never seen before stood next to Mrs. Williams at the front of the classroom. She wore denim overalls and had a clear blue backpack next to her sneakers. Her long brown hair was in a French braid, and her eyes were hazel green.

"She's pretty," Kaia said from beside them.

Lauren nodded distractedly. That wasn't the most exciting thing, though.

"Look at her backpack!" Lauren said. It was covered with little doggie faces!

"Oh, wow," Kaia breathed as they went to take their seats.

Emily grinned. "I like her already!"

Lauren couldn't wait to talk to her! She hoped the new girl would be their friend.

"Good morning, everybody," Mrs. Williams said as the kids took their seats. The teacher had a tiny metal watering can pin filled with painted flowers on her gray shirt.

Lauren took out her pencil and her notebook for Today's News.

Mrs. Williams smiled down at the new girl. "Everyone, I'm very happy to introduce you to Samantha Moore. Samantha's going to be in our class. She comes to us from the Buckeye State."

"That's Ohio," Andrew Crane shouted out. "My dad took us to a football game there."

"That Andrew thinks he knows everything," Lauren heard Emily grumble.

Samantha smiled shyly.

Mrs. Williams pointed to the empty desk kitty-corner from Emily. "Samantha, you can take a seat there."

Samantha walked over and sat down. Lauren tried to catch her eye. But Samantha kept her chin tucked down.

Mrs. Williams wrote TODAY'S NEWS on the blackboard with red chalk. Underneath she wrote:

Today is Monday, October 8.
Welcome our new friend, Samantha!

Then Mrs. Williams wrote out the week's spelling words. Lauren copied them down. As she did, she peeked over at Samantha. Samantha had opened up her doggie backpack and was taking out her pencil box.

Lauren stretched her neck to see. Cool! There was a picture of a collie on the box.

Lauren's heart started to beat faster.

Samantha was definitely a dog lover! Lauren ripped a tiny piece of paper from her journal. She wrote *Hi! I'm Lauren Parker. Want to be friends?* on the scrap. She drew a little bulldog face. Then she passed the paper forward to Samantha.

Samantha read the note and turned around. Lauren waved. Samantha waved back.

Yes! Lauren thought happily. She couldn't wait to find out if Samantha liked dogs as much as she and Emily and Kaia did—or maybe even more!

"I'm glad you're in our class," Emily told Samantha as they walked to the media center. They had introduced themselves right away.

"Thanks," Samantha said. She had a very soft voice.

"Do you miss Ohio?" Lauren asked. She thought it would be terrible to move away from all the things you liked. Your friends, your house, your school. She shivered.

Samantha nodded. "I miss my friends."

Lauren and Emily and Kaia all exchanged glances, and Lauren knew they were thinking the same thing she was.

"We'll be your friends, Samantha," Lauren said as they entered the media center.

Lauren loved it here. Her favorite part was the Reading Nook. It had a bay window. That meant the windows were curved out in a semicircle. It was very cozy. Soft, puffy cushions were propped up on the floor, and there were baskets filled with books. On the wall was a big painting of a maple tree.

Samantha looked pleased. She swung her backpack off her shoulder. "My friends call me Sam," she told them.

"My friends call me Kaia," said Kaia.

Emily giggled. "I love nicknames!" Then she frowned. "Except when they come from

Justin. He's my older brother," she told Sam. "He's always bugging us."

"I love them too," Lauren said. Her dad sometimes called her Laura Bell. But he was the only person who was allowed to call her that. The nickname was just for him to use.

"The three of us do lots of things together," Kaia explained. Emily gave a rack of books a push.

Lauren nodded. "Like play dolls."

"Ride bikes," Kaia said.

"Walk dogs," Lauren said. She gave Sam a smile. "We *love* dogs."

"And we discovered your secret!" Emily said with a canary-eating grin.

"What secret?" Sam asked, a bit bewildered.

"That you like dogs too!" Kaia said.

Sam blinked. "How . . . how do you know that?"

Lauren pointed to Sam's backpack. "This, silly! And you have a collie on your pencil box!" She looked at Emily and Kaia. "She has a collie on her pencil case."

"Cool. Do you have a collie?" Emily asked. "They're so nice."

When Sam didn't answer right away, Lauren guessed the new girl was really shy. "I have a bichon frise puppy named Coco," she added helpfully. "We're going to be in the Little Miss Maple Contest together!"

"It's a contest to celebrate our town," Kaia explained.

"I don't have a collie," Sam said. "I don't have any kind of dog." She looked at the girls. "Do you all have dogs?" she asked.

"I have a yellow Labrador puppy named Lucky," Emily told her. "I got her two weeks ago today. She's about this big"—Emily held her hands a loaf of bread apart—"and she's really lovable."

"What about you, Kaia?" Sam asked.

"I have a goldfish named Gertie. And a cat

named Purr." Kaia sighed. "But what I want more than anything on Venus is a dog."

The girls walked past the media center's display cases and the checkout desk.

"I'm going to look in the Animals and Pets section!" Emily said as she headed off.

Kaia slipped into a seat in front of a computer. "My sisters always hog our computer at home," she explained to Sam. Kaia had two sisters, one older and one younger. Lauren didn't have any. She thought it would be nice, like having a best friend who never went home. Kaia said it didn't work that way.

Lauren touched Sam's arm. "Want to look at chapter books?" she asked. "I can show you the Reading Nook."

Sam smiled. "Okay!"

Lauren loved Emily and Kaia. But having another friend was going to be nice—especially a dog lover like Sam!

Chapter Four

"Is anyone else from your class going to be in the Little Miss Maple Contest?" Lauren's mom asked.

It was after school on Tuesday. Lauren was sitting on her stool at the kitchen island, having a snack of graham crackers and milk. She wanted to give Coco a nibble. Coco wanted one, too. She kept circling Lauren's bare feet. Her small pink tongue darted in and out of her mouth. But Mommy had said no table food for Coco.

Lauren looked guiltily at Coco as she bit

into her last cracker. "Not that I know of," she mumbled through cracker crumbs. Emily and Kaia didn't like to enter contests. And Lauren hadn't heard any of the other girls at school talking about it.

Her mom lifted a bag from the counter. "I brought these things home from the shop," she said, sliding out a pile of silk leaves and flowers. "I thought I'd make you a hair wreath to go with your dress."

"Ooh, can I see?" Lauren asked, rubbing her bare toes along Coco's back. Her fur was so soft and fluffy.

Mommy brought them over. There were leaves and flowers of all different colors.

"Are you going to start now?" Lauren asked anxiously. She could hardly wait to see what her mom came up with. She was very good at arts and crafts.

Mommy gathered her long blond hair into a ponytail and fastened it with one of Lauren's elastics. "Later," she promised. "I've got to get dinner cooking. Turkey sloppy Joes and salad."

"Yum!" Lauren wiped off the graham cracker crumbs on a napkin and carefully put the leaves and flowers back in the bag.

"Will you keep an eye on Coco?" Mommy asked. "She spent all morning with me at the shop and she's pretty frisky!"

"Okay," Lauren said, hopping down from the stool. Her mom had said Coco might not listen, but if Lauren wanted to, she could enter Coco in the contest. Lauren was sure she could get Coco to listen. But they had some serious preparing to do first. "Come on, Coco! Let's go in the family room."

Playing with Coco was a lot more fun than doing chores. Lauren ran into the family room. So did Coco. Lauren lay down on the floor and Coco leapt onto her tummy.

"Remember what I told you yesterday? You're going to be in the Little Miss Maple Contest with me," Lauren said, giggling as

Coco licked her cheeks. The puppy's little white paws got tangled in Lauren's long blond hair. "Ow!" Lauren cried, giggling some more as she untangled them.

Free, Coco jumped off and ran to Lauren's feet. She gave Lauren's big toe a nip.

"Ouch! No! That's my toe, Coco!" Lauren said, liking the way the words rhymed. "If you do that onstage, I'll say 'Ho, ho, ho . . . on with the show!'" She stretched underneath the coffee table, grabbed a squeaky bone, and threw it across the room. Coco flew after it.

Pounce! Coco threw the bone up in the air. When it landed, she let out a pint-sized growl and began her attack.

Lauren rolled onto her back. Coco was going to love being the center of attention . . . and Lauren liked the spotlight too. She began to daydream. Those silk flowers Mommy had for her were really special. They were going to look so pretty with her dress!

Her dress. Her beautiful new dress. She

imagined how it looked, all ironed and perfect on the padded hanger in her closet.

Growl!

Lauren could hear her mom humming. *Mommy won't notice if I take Coco upstairs with me for a second,* she decided. She just had to see the flowers and the dress together.

Picking up Coco, she grabbed the bag of flowers Mommy had placed in the hallway and ran up to her room.

The dress hung at the front of her closet. Lauren and her mom had made a special trip to Lauren's favorite clothing store, Girlie Girl, just to pick it out.

"Look at this, Coco," she said, putting Coco on the floor. She held a bouquet of silk flowers against the dress's shimmery fabric. "Isn't this pretty? You'll wear the sweater and I'll wear this."

Lauren poufed the skirt out and twirled around the room with the dress and the flowers while Coco watched. "One two three, one two three," Lauren sang, pretending the dress was her partner in dance class. "Why, thank you," she said as she made the dress bow.

"This is called dancing, Coco," she said, doing a pirouette. Coco ran in a circle, trying to chase the little yellow, green, and orange maple leaves that flared out from the skirt.

Around and around and around. Then Lauren had a great idea. Holding the dress was fun, but it would be much more fun if she were actually *wearing* it. Kind of a trial run. Lauren bent down to give Coco a kiss, then quickly pulled off her turtleneck and jumper. Soon the soft, silky fabric was sliding over her head.

Ta-da! She spun in a circle, watching as the skirt ballooned out around her legs. Twirl and spin and curtsy and—

"Lauren! Come down here!" Mommy called. Lauren stopped in mid-pirouette. Mommy sounded angry.

Oops! Where was Coco? "What?" Lauren said, running to the banister.

Her mom stood at the foot of the stairs. Coco was running in circles around her legs. Mommy crooked her finger at Lauren. "Coco had an accident in the hallway," she said.

"How could she?" Lauren was surprised. "She was with me the whole time . . . at least, I *thought* she was. We were practicing for the contest."

Mommy frowned. "Remember what Daddy and I told you, Lauren? You need to watch Coco really carefully. As soon as she squats, whoever is there needs to scoop her up and put her on her spot."

Coco's spot was a square of newspapers laid out on the kitchen floor in front of the sliding glass doors. At night Lauren's family spread out more papers so Coco had a bigger space to go on.

"I know, but I wanted to see my dress. . . ." Lauren held up the skirt, letting the fabric slip through her fingers.

"You were supposed to be watching her,"

Mommy reminded Lauren. "I need to know I can trust you."

"Sorry," Lauren said, turning to go back to her room. But her mother stopped her.

"Not so fast," her mom said. "I won't even ask why you have on your dress. Go and change. Then I want you to clean up Coco's mess."

Lauren's face fell. "Do I have to?"

"Yes."

Lauren took a long time to take off her dress and hang it up. She took more time getting dressed. And she took even more time walking back downstairs.

But when she got there, Mommy and Coco were still waiting. "Here are some paper towels," Mommy said briskly, handing her a wad. "And this is the stain remover." She showed Lauren how to blot up the little puddle. Then she told Lauren to spray the spot with the stain remover until it was really wet.

"But don't we want the carpet to be dry?"

Lauren asked. Coco stopped running and looked at Mommy too.

"Cleaning up the puddle is just the first step," her mom explained. "Coco's sense of smell is a lot more sensitive than ours. If she smells her scent on the carpet, she'll go back to the same spot to pee again." She pointed to the bottle. "This will help get rid of the smell so Coco won't want to go here again."

Mommy went back into the kitchen. Coco ran after her. Lauren took a big breath, then sprayed the stain remover on the spot and covered it with a plastic garbage bag so it would stay wet. Mommy said they had to leave it like that for a whole day.

Then Lauren eyeballed the wet paper towels. *Yuck!* This was gross.

Coco came scurrying back in and sat down beside her. She looked at Lauren, a curious expression on her fluffy white face.

"You've got to go to the bathroom outside, Coco," Lauren begged. "I love you, but I *hate* cleaning up after you!" she said with a sigh, reaching out for the wet paper towels.

Coco stood up. Then she started to sit back down. But she didn't. Coco wasn't sitting. She was squatting! "Not again," Lauren cried, scooping her puppy up and running with her to the kitchen.

She had to train Coco to listen to her every command. They only had a few days before the contest!

Just a Li'l Pawprint from Coco

All that twirling and spinning Lauren was doing in her dress made me dizzy. That's why I ran downstairs. I was worried. What if she started spinning me like that? I don't think I would like it.

And what does "false alarm" mean? That's what Lauren's mommy said when Lauren finally lifted me off that paper with all the writing on it. Everyone keeps telling me that paper is my spot. What does it mean? What am I supposed to do?

C.

Chapter Five

"Sam! Over here," Kaia called, waving the new girl over to their lunch table.

"Wake up, Lauren," Emily said, elbowing her in the ribs.

Embarrassed, Lauren tried to sit up straight. When she felt another yawn coming, she covered her mouth. She'd been yawning ever since school started—and it wasn't even noon!

Coco had whimpered and cried all night. Lauren had taken her out early that morning, hoping to train her for the contest. But Coco had run around the yard like the frisky puppy she was. Daddy had to step in.

Sam walked over, balancing a grilled cheese sandwich, French fries, and milk carton on her tray. She looked happy to see them.

Kaia patted the seat beside her. "Yesterday you sat by Lauren. Sit by me today."

"Ooh, you got the grilled cheese too," Emily said, pointing to Sam's sandwich. "They toast them just right."

"There's so much to choose from," Sam said, sliding into the seat next to Kaia. "Even tacos!"

"I'm so tired!" Lauren mumbled, yawning again. "I never realized how much work went into taking care of a dog."

Emily groaned. "Puppies are work, work, work! My parents told me Lucky needs to learn that the *people* in our family are in charge. Not her."

"Even people like Justin?" Kaia asked, sipping from her juice box.

Emily scowled. "Yeah. But even he thinks housetraining a puppy is hard. And it does take a few nights for puppies to get over their homesickness," she said knowingly. "But it's worth it, isn't it?"

Lauren took out some Polaroids she had in her book bag. Coco's small round eyes and puffball hairdo stared back at her. Her heart melted. "It is." She showed Sam the photos. "Isn't she the cutest?" she asked, brushing the crumbs from the table before setting the pictures down. "See her paws?"

Sam studied a photograph. "They're so little."

"Now that Lauren has Coco and I have Lucky, we're one step closer to our dog club," Emily said.

Lauren looked guiltily at Sam. Was it mean to talk about their club in front of her?

"We've been planning the club for a few weeks but we haven't held any meetings yet," Emily went on. "We wanted to wait until Kaia got her dog too."

"My mom *has* to let me get a dog if I'm in a dog club," Kaia explained to Sam.

Sam didn't look upset, so Lauren decided it was okay to go on. "I've been thinking of stuff we could do," she said. She held up the pictures. "That's why I took these. I thought maybe we could make up little cards with pictures of our dogs and us on them. When we arrive at club meetings, we'll have to show the card to get in."

"But won't we recognize you?" Kaia asked.

Lauren giggled. "I hope so. I just thought it would be cute."

"Okay," Kaia said, pulling little pieces of her curly hair over her shoulders. "Let's do it."

Sam stopped chewing, holding her grilled cheese sandwich in midair. "You know what? My mom said once we settle into our new house, we're going to get a dog too."

"Cool!" Kaia said.

"What kind?" asked Lauren.

"Oh, we're not sure yet," Sam said.

"If you have any questions about dogs, just ask me," Emily told her. "Not to brag, but I know a lot about dogs."

"She does, and she's not bragging," Kaia said.

Lauren crossed her fingers. She didn't want to say anything to Sam without making sure Emily and Kaia felt the same way. But if Sam got a dog, she would be eligible to join their dog club!

And that was exactly what Lauren wanted to happen!

Chapter Six

100%—Great Job!

Math Quiz

Name: <u>Lauren Parker, Room 302</u>

Add the following:

+ 302	+ 601	+ 799
124	222	129
426	823	928

+ 558	+ 336	+ 817
100	425	602
658	761	1419

Lauren skipped all the way up the walk after Emily and Mrs. Conner dropped her off. She still couldn't believe she'd gotten a hundred on her math quiz. That was her best math grade ever!

"Mommy?" Lauren called, unlocking the front door. She could hear Coco's paws prancing around on the kitchen floor.

"I'm on the phone with the shop, honey," her mom called, poking her head out of the living room. She blew Lauren a kiss. "I'll be off in a sec."

"Okay. I'll take Coco out."

Coco would go crazy if she saw her, so, making sure the coast was clear, Lauren ran upstairs. She changed into her brown corduroys and a cream top with a tulip on it. "I'll have just enough time to grab a snack and play with Coco," she told herself as she went down to the kitchen. "Then it'll be time to meet Emily and Kaia and walk Brighton."

"Hi, little Coco," she said, dropping to her knees. Coco covered her face with licks. "I missed you, too!" Lauren giggled as she saw what her mom had left on the table—a glass of milk, a granola bar, and a pile of small dog biscuits.

"Now, let's see. Which snack is mine?" Lauren pretended to wonder, ripping open the granola bar's wrapper. She picked up the doggie biscuits, got Coco's leash, and opened the sliding glass doors. Coco trotted outside behind her.

"Okay, Coco, time to go," Lauren said, picking Coco up and putting her on the grass next to the patio.

And Coco went!

"Good girl, good girl!" Lauren cried, giving her a doggie biscuit.

Coco wagged her tail. Then she was off. She barked at an imaginary bird. She ran over and sniffed the flowers. She tried to hop up into the birdbath, but her legs were too short.

Lauren chased the puppy. "Come and get me, Coco," she said, running across the lawn. Coco flew after her. Lauren stopped. She dropped to the ground. She pretended to be asleep.

Soon a little wet nose sniffed her ear. And a little wet tongue licked her neck. "Okay, okay, I'm awake!" Lauren said, rolling over and tickling Coco.

Coco lay down and showed her belly to Lauren. "Oh, do you want me to scratch you?" Lauren asked, lightly rubbing the soft white tummy curls. Coco sighed happily.

Everything was going great. So great that Lauren decided to try a little experiment. "Okay, Coco. Get up."

Coco hopped to her feet.

"Follow me, Coco," Lauren ordered, running into the middle of the yard.

Coco followed.

"Good girl!" Lauren clipped the leash onto her collar. "Okay, Coco. Sit," Lauren said, taking a doggie biscuit, putting it in front of Coco's face, and then quickly moving it behind the puppy's head. Her dad had taught her that trick.

Coco sat and turned her head to reach the

biscuit. "Good girl!" Lauren said, handing her the treat.

Coco gobbled it up.

Then Lauren lay down.

Coco lay down.

"Good girl!" Lauren said, flipping her puppy another doggie biscuit. This proved it—Coco was on her way to a perfect show at the Little Miss Maple Contest!

Mommy was still on the phone when Lauren brought Coco back inside. Lauren tucked Coco under her arm and tiptoed up to her room. As long as Coco had done her business, Lauren told herself, there wasn't a problem with bringing her upstairs.

Coco ran around and sniffed Lauren's things. Lauren wanted to pick her up and kiss her over and over, but she didn't want to annoy her.

"I know what we should do," Lauren said after Coco had checked everything out. "I need to brush your hair!" Would Mommy let her brush Coco's hair in the house? "Well, I brush my hair in here," Lauren said out loud. "Why not your hair?" She kissed Coco's nose and put her on top of the bed. "I'll be right back. Stay, Coco. You stay."

Lauren hurried downstairs. Where was Coco's brush? She looked in the laundry room. The garage. Even in the cabinet under the kitchen sink. Then she remembered. She had left the brush out on the patio yesterday. Sure enough, that was where it was. She wiped it off with her hand and ran back to her room.

Coco looked up at her when she walked in. Her mouth was covered with black fuzz. Not just carpet fuzz or sock fuzz . . . it was the black fuzz of Shamu, the stuffed whale Lauren got the summer before at Sea World!

"Nooooo!" Lauren cried, warm tears filling her eyes. She loved Shamu!

But that wasn't all. Coco had knocked over a pile of folded laundry that sat on Lauren's desk.

And there were little soggy shredded bits of paper on the floor. Lauren picked the biggest one up. "Oh, no." She gasped. This was no ordinary paper—it was her math test! Except now it was wet. And it didn't say *Great Job* anymore. Now it said *eat Jo*.

"Oh, Coco," Lauren wailed.

"What's going on in here?" Mommy asked, walking in. She took in the confusion. "Uh-oh."

"She ate Shamu, Mommy," Lauren said tearfully, pointing at Coco. Coco wagged her tail. "She knocked over the laundry, too, *and* she chewed up my math test. I got a hundred." Lauren held out the mushy paper. "See?"

"Honey, that's wonderful!" Mommy gave Lauren a hug. "I'm sorry I was on the phone for so long. But it's because of a scene like this that we told you Coco has to stay in the kitchen until she gets bigger."

"I just wanted to brush her," Lauren whispered as the bichon frise came over to lick her hand. She knew Coco didn't know any better. But it was frustrating!

"That was nice, but Coco is a puppy, and sometimes puppies make messes, especially when they're left alone." Mommy whisked Coco up. "Promise me this is the last time I'll find her up here. Okay?"

Lauren rubbed her eyes. "Okay." Coco's puffy white head bobbed up and down as her mom walked away. With a sniffle, Lauren began picking up what was left of Shamu. *This stuffing was probably from Shamu's head,* she thought, holding a clump. *And this stuffing was from Shamu's tail.* She loved Coco a lot—but she was kind of upset with her right now. Her favorite stuffed animal and her test were ruined. And at this rate, so were her chances of winning the competition!

Chapter Seven

"So that's what happened," Lauren said later as she and her friends rounded the corner onto Ivy Street. "Coco went loco."

Emily was letting Lauren hold Brighton's leash. Brighton was an Airedale terrier. He belonged to Emily's English neighbor, Mr. Virley. Mr. Virley paid Emily to walk Brighton twice a week, and Lauren and Kaia joined them when they could.

Brighton was very handsome. He was fluffy and tan, and he was always smiling. At least Lauren thought he was.

"I still think you should bring her to the Little Miss Maple Contest," Kaia said. "No one else will have a dog half as cute."

"Or as funny!" Emily laughed, and so did Kaia.

"But what if she goes crazy *there*?" Lauren worried aloud. Sure, her friends could think it was funny. They weren't the ones who would be up onstage! "I'd be so embarrassed!" She stared down at her sneaker shoelaces. Her shoes had been brand new just a few weeks before—but the laces were all chewed up, thanks to Coco. *Not even my shoelaces are safe,* Lauren thought.

"She might surprise you," Kaia said, skipping through a pile of leaves. "She might clam up."

"Some dogs put their tails between their legs when they get scared or worried," Emily said as they neared Greenside Park.

Lauren was handing the leash back to Emily when a flash of pink caught her eye. "Hey, look! There's Sam," she said. Samantha was standing at the park's entrance, bouncing a pink rubber ball.

"Sam!" Kaia yelled. Sam looked up, startled. Then she waved.

Emily, Kaia, Lauren, and Brighton ran toward her.

"Hi," the girls said together, breathless. Brighton gave a short bark.

"I thought you had a Labrador retriever," Sam said to Emily. She stepped back a little. "A puppy."

"I do! She's home. This is Brighton," Emily said, patting his head. "He's an Airedale terrier. I'm his dog walker."

"Oh." Sam fiddled with the end of her braid. "So you kind of have two dogs. That's a lot to handle."

Emily laughed. "It sure will be fun when Brighton and Lucky and Coco all meet."

"Do you want to come and play Frisbee with us?" Kaia asked, showing the Airedale's chewed-up toy to Sam. "Brighton is so funny.

He waits until you throw it, then he takes off and—"

Sam shook her head really fast. "I—I was just going. My mom's expecting me home."

"Oh, okay," said Emily. Lauren could tell she was disappointed. And so was Lauren. She wanted to get to know Sam better. She had been thinking of asking her friends something really important, and it would have helped to know Sam better. Still . . .

"Do you live around here?" Lauren asked.

Sam nodded. "On Oakdale Road. The white house with blue shutters."

"We're neighbors!" Emily declared. "Kaia and I live on Ivy Street."

"I live close too, on Holly Avenue," Lauren added. "Maybe you can come over and play one day. And meet Coco!"

"Sure," Sam said. She smiled. "I'd better go. Bye." She took off.

"I like her," Emily said, unclipping Brighton's leash. He was allowed to run free in the park if there weren't other people around. "I sat next to her in art. She's nice."

"And smart," Lauren said. "Did you guys see how she knew all the answers to Mrs. Williams's questions?"

"But she isn't a show-off," Kaia pointed out, tossing the Frisbee. Brighton tore after it.

"She's shy," Emily said. "She needs some friends."

Lauren looked at each of her friends. "Were you guys thinking what I was thinking?" she asked, crossing her fingers and imagining crossing her toes.

"Are you thinking you want to invite her to be part of our club?" Kaia asked eagerly.

"That's what I was thinking," Emily said happily.

"We're thinking alike again!" Lauren said. Her dad had told them that they had been friends for so long that their brains worked like one giant brain. Lauren wished that were true when it came to schoolwork.

Brighton came running back. *"Ruff!"*

"He agrees with us too," Kaia said, patting his head.

"So when do you think we should ask her?" Emily wanted to know.

Lauren picked up the Frisbee and let it sail off. "I say the sooner the better."

"We could run after her right now," Kaia said, squinting in the direction Sam had gone.

Emily shook her head. "That makes it look like maybe we're just doing it because she was all alone. We can ask her tomorrow morning."

"Three people is barely a club, after all," Lauren said. "But four is the perfect number of members!"

Emily linked her right arm in Lauren's left. Lauren linked her right arm in Kaia's left. And Kaia linked her right arm in Emily's left. Brighton was squished between their feet.

Lauren put her blond head against Emily's glossy brown hair and Kaia's springy black curls. Whenever they made a decision that affected all of them, they huddled together. And did some fast thinking.

"So we agree—" Emily started.

"No more three!" Lauren said.

"For dogs galore, our club has—" Kaia began.

"Four!" they all shouted.

Chapter Eight

"**A**re you ready?" Lauren asked Kaia after her mom dropped her off at school. Lauren smoothed down her jumper and tightened her pigtail holders. She wanted to look as official as possible. After all, they had very official business to discuss.

"Sure as shootin'," Kaia said, clicking her clogs together. "Is Emily here?"

Lauren nodded. "She went to find Sam."

Curly Maple Elementary School was always crazy in the morning. Moms and dads double-parking. Kids playing. Teachers talking.

"Guys! Here we are," Emily called, running over to them. She had Sam by the elbow. Sam looked curious.

"Since it was your idea, I think you should tell her," Emily said, poking Lauren with her finger.

Lauren felt shy. "No, you," she told Kaia, nudging her.

Kaia took a deep breath. Then she shook her head. "We *all* want her to. So we *all* have to ask her."

"We want you to join our dog club!" they shouted.

"You do?" Sam asked, looking at each of them.

They nodded.

"We're going to do lots of fun things," Lauren assured her.

"And we aren't letting just anyone join," Emily said, lowering her voice. "It's for people like us."

Kaia pointed to Sam's backpack. "People who live for and dream of dogs!"

Sam giggled. Then her face got kind of serious, as if she was thinking about it. She licked her lips. "Okay! Count me in!"

"Whew, it's a good thing you said yes," Lauren said, grinning. "Because I already made you one of these." She took an envelope out of her backpack. Inside were four bright pink cards. They were the same size as the photos Lauren's mom got of Lauren at the mall.

"You made membership cards!" Emily looked impressed.

Lauren didn't tell her friends that she'd had to throw the first set away after Coco bit into it. Instead, she handed the top card to Emily.

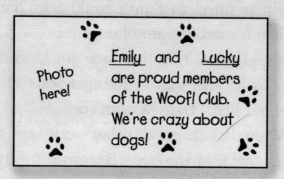

Photo here!

Emily and Lucky are proud members of the Woof! Club. We're crazy about dogs!

"The Woof! Club?" Kaia said as Lauren handed her a card too. It was just like Emily's, except the place where the dog's name went was blank.

"Do you like it?" Lauren asked, giving a card to Sam. She and her mom had thought the name was cute, but everyone had to agree on it or else it wouldn't be fair. "Here's my card," she added, showing her friends the adorable photo of her and Coco that she had glued down.

"The picture is great!" Emily said. "And so are these cards. You did a really nice job."

"Will we have club meetings?" Sam asked, tucking her card between the pages of a book.

"Pronto," Kaia told her.

"Could we wait until the Little Miss Maple Contest is over?" Lauren asked hopefully. "I've got a lot to do before Saturday."

Everyone thought that was fair.

Lauren wanted to show them what she had in her backpack—her mom had finished her hair wreath and had let her take it to school. But *brring!* There was no time now. The morning bell rang again and Emily, Kaia, Lauren, and Sam lined up.

Thursday mornings were always exciting for room 302. Instead of Today's News, it was Show & Look! Today was Zoe Cho's turn. She had made a papier-mâché bowl with her mom.

Seeing everyone's excited faces when Zoe showed them the bowl made Lauren even more anxious to show her wreath to her friends.

My friends in the Woof! Club, she thought happily.

After Show & Look, they had language arts. Then came music, where they listened to a CD of a "mean fiddle player." That was what their music teacher, Mr. Root, said. Then lunch. When the class was through eating, Mrs. Williams let them out on the playground. Lauren gathered her friends around her by the monkey bars.

"I brought this to show you guys," she said, unzipping her backpack. She carefully lifted out the wreath. It was made of twigs and had little yellow and orange and green leaves glued to it.

Or at least, it used to have.

"Um, what is that?" Emily asked as Lauren held up the wreath. All but a few leaves were gone, and some of the twigs had snapped in half. A gum wrapper was stuck to a twig.

"It's my hair wreath for the contest," Lauren wailed. An orange leaf fluttered to the ground.

"Are you sure you want to put that in your hair?" Kaia asked. "You could borrow some of my ponytail holders if you want."

Lauren couldn't figure out what had happened. It had looked perfect when she put it in her backpack the night before. And she'd been careful not to squish it in the car.

"Is that part of the wreath?" Sam asked, pointing to a little brown nugget in Lauren's backpack zipper pocket.

Emily bent down to look. "Mystery solved! It's Coco's dog food! Puppies get into everything."

"Coco probably thought she was playing a game," Kaia said, examining the wreath. "This does kind of look like something you'd find in the park. You know, leaves and twigs."

Game? Now wasn't the time for games. The contest was in two days! In fact, Coco was going to the groomer's that day to get bathed and brushed. "I hope my mom can fix this," Lauren said, tugging at both her pigtails in frustration. She loved her wreath the way it had looked before. But now she'd rather have a bird's nest on her head!

That darn Coco. Would her bichon ever be ready for the contest?

And more importantly, would Lauren?

Chapter Nine

After dinner on Thursday night, Lauren and her dad drove over to Bow Wow Beauty.

"Someone's eager to see you," the groomer said with a smile when they walked in. She wore an apron that said QUIT YER BARKIN', and she smelled like shampoo.

"I'm eager too!" Lauren declared. She had been looking for Coco since the second they walked into the busy pet salon. Dogs of all shapes and sizes were there. A Yorkie with a bright bow was tucked under his owner's arm. A big sheepdog waited patiently for the boy who was with her to tie his shoes. A shaggy honey-colored pooch peeked at Lauren from behind his silky hair.

Lauren held her dad's hand as a teenage boy came out of a back room. In his arms was a gleaming white puffball. "Coco!" Lauren shrieked, burying her face in her puppy's silky hair. "You look like a movie star!"

"She's a very stylish young lady," the groomer told Lauren. "We trimmed around her eyes and ears and brushed her out."

Lauren giggled. "She looks like a cloud!"

"Somehow I don't think we're going to be able to keep her looking like that," Daddy said as he paid the bill.

"Bichons need a lot of upkeep," the groomer agreed.

"I thought she would have a bow in her hair," Lauren said, looking over at the Yorkie.

"Normally we don't put bows on bichons," the groomer explained, giving Coco a good-bye pat.

"Well, she sure couldn't get any cuter," Lauren said.

"I feel like showing off my two pretty girls," Daddy said as they got into the car. "Anyone feel like an ice cream?"

"I do!" Lauren said, giggling at how Daddy had called Coco his girl. Lauren always loved going places with him. He made everything fun. Not that Mommy wasn't fun too. But somehow being out with just Daddy made everything seem like an adventure.

Soda Pop's had the best ice cream in Lakeville. The people who worked there were nice, too—they let Coco sit at a booth!

"Here, Coco. Stay," Lauren coaxed, trying to look at a menu. Photos of strawberry parfaits and hot fudge sundaes and ice cream sandwiches made her mouth water. "Don't these all look yummy?" she said out loud.

Coco was busy sniffing and licking. Her nails scrambled back and forth on the bench.

"Kids probably spilled ice cream here and

Coco smells it even though it's cleaned up," Lauren told her dad. Coco lay down on the seat and rested her head in Lauren's lap.

"Maybe being at the groomer tired her out," Daddy said. After they ordered, he leaned forward and smiled at Lauren. "So how's school, honey?"

"Peachy," Lauren said. Kaia had taught her that word. "There's a new girl in my class, Samantha. Everyone calls her Sam. She's going to be in the Woof! Club."

"The what club?" Daddy looked confused.

Lauren explained about their new dog club. "I might need to use the computer sometimes," she said. "You know, if we have newsletters or something."

"Just let me know." Daddy reached over and tweaked her nose. "With the big news about your club, are you still excited about the contest?"

Lauren nodded. "Yes, but I'm kind of worried about Coco. She acts so silly sometimes.

What if she runs away from me? Or has an accident? Or . . . or nips someone in the leg?"

Daddy peered over the table. Coco was curled up into a little ball. "There's no predicting how she'll be. She's a dog!" He tilted his head. "If she does act up, you'll just have to take charge, Lauren. She's going to be your responsibility that day."

Lauren sat up straighter. "I know. That's what got me worried in the first place!"

Just then Coco stirred. Her dark eyes peeked over the edge of the table. Her round black nose sniffed the air.

"What a wittle cream puff!" the waitress cooed when she brought out their floats. Daddy had a chocolate one. Lauren had root beer.

"Is that a poodle?" asked a boy from the booth behind them.

"How old is he?" asked an elderly lady.

"What's your dog's name?" asked a set of red-haired twins.

"Can she have some of this?" asked Brittany, a girl from Lauren's class. She held out her ice cream cone.

Lauren was spending so much time answering all the questions that she couldn't even finish her float.

"Her name is Coco and she's a bichon frise," she said for the fifteenth time, this time to a young couple with a baby. She sighed. "This is exasperating, Daddy," she said, going to take a sip of her float.

"Hey!" she cried. Someone had already been sipping! Root beer and ice cream dribbled down Coco's tiny white chin.

Lauren buried her head in her hands. Then she pulled a napkin from the dispenser, dipped it in her ice water, and began dabbing at Coco.

"I guess she likes root beer," Daddy said with a smile.

"See what I meant about acting crazy?" Lauren moaned.

Daddy winked. "I sure do. How could anyone prefer root beer over chocolate?"

Just a Li'l Pawprint from Coco

My mommy Lauren can't talk anymore! She keeps saying the same
things to me. Over and over. Day after
day! She calls it our training session. I
call it boring!

"Come!"

"Sit!"

"Lie down!"

"Roll over!"

"Still and quiet! S and Q!"

If I do what she says, she gives me a
biscuit and says "Good girl!" If I don't do
what she says, she looks real sad. But, see,
sometimes I'm not hungry! I don't want a
biscuit! So I don't do what she wants.

But I don't want her to be sad. So I try
to make her laugh. I run around. I do
flips! I lick her face!

Anything not to get a biscuit.

(Unless they're the beef-flavored kind.)

C.

Chapter Ten

"This one is even prettier than my last, if I do say so myself," Mommy declared as Lauren put the new wreath on her head. Lauren looked at herself in her bedroom mirror. This wreath was made from twigs and leaves too, but Mommy had added some fake berries and moss.

"I say so too," Lauren said. Boy, was she relieved!

Coco let out a bark. "So does Coco," Lauren said, scooping her up and kissing her.

"Now, I don't want you to make a habit of coming into Lauren's bedroom, but this is a special occasion, Coco," Mommy said. She lifted up a smaller version of Lauren's wreath and placed it on Coco's head.

Lauren squealed. "She's cute as a button!"

Mommy laughed as Lauren held Coco under her front paws and lifted her up to the mirror. "Coco, look how cute you are. See?"

Coco tilted her head to the left. Then to the right.

"She likes it!" Lauren said excitedly. Then Coco shook her head. The wreath slid onto her nose.

"Oh no you don't," Mommy said, rescuing the wreath from Coco's tiny teeth. "I'm not making another one of these, too!"

"We'd better put that away until tomorrow," Lauren told her mom, removing her wreath.

"Good idea." Mommy wrapped the wreaths in green tissue paper and put them on the closet shelf. The three of them went downstairs to the kitchen.

Coco ran over to her beanbag bed, the one

Emily had helped pick out at Pet Parade. When she turned around, something orange was in her mouth. *Squeak! Squeak!*

"She plays with that toy all day," Mommy said, pointing to the orange squeaky toy Emily had surprised Coco with.

"Maybe I should bring it with me to the Little Miss Maple Contest," Lauren said. "I want her to be as calm as possible."

"Having Coco in the contest might be more than you bargained for, sweetie," Mommy reminded her. They sat down at the island.

"I suppose, but . . ." Lauren trailed off. She slid down from her stool. "I'll prove to you that Coco has what it takes! Okay, Coco. Show us what you've got."

Lauren crouched. "Coco. Lie down. Lie down."

Coco looked confused.

Lauren patted the kitchen floor. "Coco. Like this." She lay on the tiles. Coco hopped onto Lauren's tummy and wagged her tail.

Mommy laughed. "That's how you listened to me when you were a baby."

"Kiss me, Coco!" Lauren said. She tilted her face and Coco licked her cheek. That was an easy one, but she needed *something* positive to go on.

Lauren wiped her face and sat up. "Coco. Get your toy!" She threw the orange squeaky across the room. Coco ran after it.

Lauren waited. Coco ran with the toy over to the dishwasher.

"Here, Coco. To me," Lauren said.

Coco listened! She brought the toy back, dropping it at Lauren's feet.

"That's a good girl!" Lauren said, patting her head. Then she scooted across the room. "Come here, Coco. Come!" She held out a small bone.

"Good job, Lauren," Mommy said encouragingly. "Coco's learning to come to you when you call her."

Then Mommy and Lauren worked to put

the pretty collar on Coco that they had bought for her at Pet Parade. Coco's fluffy white paws clawed at the air.

"Coco wants the collar off," Lauren said. "I think this one's itchy." She put her hands around her own neck. Wearing a collar wouldn't be fun at all.

Mommy gave the puppy another bone-shaped biscuit. "We need to distract her. Soon she won't even think about the collar."

Sure enough, Coco became so busy with the biscuit that she forgot all about the collar.

That's because Coco is smart, Lauren thought happily. Sure, her puppy wasn't perfect yet, but she was a quick learner. She was going to do just fine on Saturday!

Lauren snuggled under her flowered sheets. "Just one more story?" she begged her dad.

"Maybe the one about the princess who wants to travel around the world on her scooter?"

He shook his head. "Two's the limit. You know that."

"I know," she grumbled, pulling her blanket up so the satin hem touched her chin.

Mommy sat down and stroked her cheek. "We want you to get a good night's sleep tonight so you're all ready for your big day tomorrow."

"I can't wait," Lauren told them. "This is the first time I've ever competed with a pet!"

"Well, remember, Laura Bell," Dad said, "it doesn't matter if you win or lose." He always said that before Lauren entered a competition.

"We just want you to have fun," Mommy said. She always said that before Lauren entered a competition.

"I know," Lauren said. She always said that before she entered a competition. She believed it too. Still, she couldn't help letting her eyes travel up to her special shelf. Tap dancing, gymnastics, crafts . . . wouldn't it be swell to get another trophy to put up there?

A trophy she and Coco won *together*.

Chapter Eleven

"**C**heck it out!" Kaia said as they walked through the entrance of the Lakeville Festival Grounds. There were people everywhere. The trees that circled the grounds had just started to change color.

"They've got butterfly fries!" Emily said excitedly, pointing to a stand.

"And candied apples!" Sam added, licking her lips.

"I'm so glad you guys could come with me," Lauren said. She took a deep breath and gazed around them. Quilt displays and cider press demonstrations . . . petting zoos and country crafts . . . hot apple cider and fresh-cooked doughnuts . . . the place was swarming with activity!

But the biggest and most exciting thing was the Little Miss Maple Contest! Straight ahead of them was a banner painted in orange and gold. WELCOME, LITTLE MISS MAPLE CONTESTANTS! it said. Below it was Maple Court, the stage where the contestants would strut their stuff. Stereo speakers stood on the sides, and the platform was decorated with artificial leaves.

"Okay, girls, let's get Lauren signed in, then we'll make the rounds," Daddy said. He grinned at Emily. "I'm a sucker for butterfly fries myself."

Lauren held Coco close against her chest as they all walked to the sign-in table.

Lauren was already registered. All she had to do now was print her name on a piece of paper.

"Here you go, little lady," said the curly-haired woman in charge as she rummaged through a stack of cards with big numbers written on them and pulled out the number 16. She clipped the card to Lauren's dress.

"What about this little lady?" Lauren asked, holding up Coco, who was dressed in her special maple leaf sweater and wreath.

"Oh, why, of course we can't forget her," the woman said. She fished around until she found a smaller tag that said 16. It hung from a cord, and the woman put it around Coco's neck.

Coco looked perplexed.

"Now, just go over to that area marked with the green balloons and wait until they call your number," the woman instructed. "Next?" she said, moving on to the girl behind Lauren.

Emily, Kaia, and Sam each gave Lauren and Coco a hug. "You go, girl," Emily told her.

"Keep going until you win!" Kaia added, pumping her fist.

"Good luck, Lauren," Sam said shyly. She slipped a small gold ring off her finger and onto Lauren's. "Wear this for luck."

Lauren's friends moved back as her mom crouched down. "Looks like this is it," Mommy whispered, straightening the pleats of Lauren's new dress. "Any monarchs?"

Lauren shook her head. "Not even any moths!" She kissed her parents good-bye, waved to her friends, and, with Coco under her arm, headed off toward the balloons.

"We love you!" Mommy called.

Love you, too, Lauren thought.

A bunch of girls Lauren's age stood by the green balloons. Lauren walked up to them.

"Hi," she said. She liked making friends at competitions. It helped her be less nervous when her turn came.

"Is this your first contest?" Number 8, a girl with cornrows and a hat dripping with leaves, asked her.

"No," Lauren said. "But it's my first time with Coco." She held out her puppy. "How about you?"

The girl nodded. "I'm so nervous!"

"Don't be scared," said Number 14, a tall blond girl carrying a basket. A basket that Coco started sniffing.

"What do you have in there?" Lauren asked, trying to peek.

The girl lifted the gingham cloth. Pancakes . . . and maple syrup!

"Ooh, don't let my dog see that," Lauren said, covering Coco's eyes and nose. "You won't have any left for the competition!

"There sure are a lot of girls here, Coco," Lauren whispered into Coco's fluffy ear. "And some funny pets, too!" She'd spotted a ferret, a parakeet, and a tiny black kitten!

"I was going to bring my Samoyed, Bronco, but I didn't think he'd listen to me," said Number 3, a girl wearing a white T-shirt with a red maple leaf on it. She carried a matching umbrella.

Lauren smiled. "I've been training Coco for days," she said, petting Coco gently. The bichon nestled into her arms. She was being so good! Lauren let out a deep sigh of relief. What on earth had she been worried about?

A few seconds later a man wearing a vest patterned with leaves and carrying a clipboard motioned for everyone to gather around.

"Attention, Maplettes!" he said, snapping his fingers three times. "I want you to line up in numerical order. When it's your turn, you will walk down Maple Court for our judges. When you reach the end of the court, please turn, hold your pose, and then walk back. Our stage is a basic rectangle marked with three X's across the front. If you have a pet, it can walk beside you or you may carry it."

Lauren looked toward Maple Court. A big crowd had formed. For a moment she thought she saw Kaia's purple turtleneck, but she wasn't sure.

The man smiled at them. "Good luck, everybody!"

Lauren found her place between Numbers 15 and 17. "This is it, Coco Puff," she said softly, adjusting their wreaths. "Time to shine!"

She fluffed out her skirt.

She fluffed out her hair.

She fluffed out Coco's head and legs.

She was ready.

The sounds of musical instruments and singing drifted down to her ears. As they moved closer to the steps, Lauren saw that a small band was playing on the stage.

"Hear the music, Coco?" Lauren asked as Number 15 walked down Maple Court, keeping time with the beat.

Coco looked the way Number 15 did. She was wriggling and squirming and . . . trying to dance!

"No, Coco, no dancing," Lauren whispered as Number 15 made her way back. "Remember, you need to stay still and quiet. S and Q!"

Lauren walked up the small staircase and out onto the stage. All eyes were on her and Coco.

She smiled her brightest smile. Her dress was perfect. Her wreath was perfect. And Coco was perfect.

For almost four seconds.

Then Coco leapt from Lauren's arms. "Coco!" Lauren whispered as loudly as she dared. In horror, she watched as Coco rolled like a furry snowball to the left. Then she spun like a leaf in the wind to the right.

Normally Lauren was poised. Normally she had what adults called "presence." But right now the only P-word that described her was *panicked!*

In the middle of all the commotion, Lauren suddenly thought, *Her wreath!* Where was Coco's wreath? Part of it was on the stage. Part of it had blown off in the breeze. A few stray twigs were stuck in the fur on her head.

The band started to play a song Lauren had heard at a wedding, "The Electric Slide."

Coco started to dance. Or maybe it was a

wiggle. Whatever it was, she quickly got her little legs free from the maple leaf sweater, and it soon inched up around her neck.

"*Yip!*" Coco let out a bark and tried to twist out of the sweater altogether. "*Yip!*"

The band stopped "The Electric Slide" . . . and started "The Twist!"

The crowd went wild . . . Coco *was* wild. When Coco gave up on the sweater and scampered toward the judges, Lauren scampered after her. She had a contest to finish and still had to walk to the end and smile!

Lauren didn't feel much like smiling . . . in fact, she felt like boo-hooing. *My dress, my wreath, my chance to win Little Miss Maple and get that trophy . . . it's all ruined,* she thought, a hiccup catching in her throat. But then she spotted Emily, Kaia, and Sam in the crowd.

"Whoo-hoo!" Emily yelled, her hands cupping her mouth. Kaia was cheering. Sam was waving.

They looked like they were having fun!

They were laughing, but not *at* her. *With* her. That is, if she was willing to laugh too.

Taking a deep breath, Lauren raced forward, grabbed Coco, and smiled down at the judges. Even if she was going to lose, she would still give it her best. Her friends had given her the courage she needed to go on.

Static shot through the speakers. "Thank you for a most entertaining walk, Number 16," Mr. Hurley, owner of Hurley's Home Repairs, said into his microphone.

With a small bow, Lauren scooted back down Maple Court. Coco licked her face. Then the puppy nestled back in her arms, her little chest heaving.

"Sure, *now* you're tired," Lauren said, trudging down the stairs.

Lauren's worst fears had come true: Coco had definitely gone loco.

Just a Li'l Pawprint from Coco

What was that all about?

C.

Chapter Twelve

"**W**e were awful," Lauren moaned to her friends. The competition had ended, and now everyone was waiting eagerly for the results.

"You rocked!" Kaia insisted. "I got a great picture of you doing a belly-flop dive after Coco."

Emily pushed back her headband. "I give you a ten for effort, energy, and entertainment!"

"Everyone will remember you," Sam said optimistically before she bit into her candied apple.

Lauren cuddled Coco and tried to be positive. Mommy and Daddy had hugged her hard, laughed a little, and told her that whatever happened, they'd never forget the first Little Miss Maple Contest.

"Here comes a judge," Emily burst out.

Lauren took off Sam's ring and handed it back. "Thanks anyway," she whispered.

It was Mrs. Delarosa. She worked at the doughnut shop.

A hush fell over the crowd as Mrs. Delarosa approached the microphone on the stage.

"First let me say how much we appreciate all our Little Miss Maple contestants. You were wonderful!" She clapped heartily. "All our winners will receive trophies, as well as some special gifts." She paused. "So, without further ado, our second runner-up, and the winner of a dozen doughnuts from my shop and a twenty-five-dollar gift certificate to Girlie Girl, is Number 14, Veronica Lee!" It was the maple syrup girl. Lauren applauded as Veronica accepted her award.

"Our first runner-up, and winner of a pizza from Vinnie's Pizza and a fifty-dollar gift certificate to the Toy Shop, is Number 2, Charity Anderson!" A girl wearing a tree costume waddled up to the stage.

"She must really have wanted to win," Emily whispered, putting her arm around Lauren.

Lauren nodded, looking at Coco. She knew winning wasn't everything . . . but somehow, because she had entered with Coco, winning would have been extra-special.

"And, now, the moment you've all been waiting for." Mrs. Delarosa beamed. "The winner of our first annual Little Miss Maple Contest—and the recipient of a yellow slicker and rubber boots for herself and her pooch from It's Raining, It's Pouring along with a hundred-dollar gift certificate to Pet Parade, is someone who remained confident even though things got a little crazy. It's our Number 16s, Lauren and Coco Parker!"

Lauren gasped as her friends threw their arms around her. "You won!" they shouted amid the applause.

"We won, Coco!" Lauren squealed. "We won!" She hurried up to the stage, where Mrs. Delarosa handed her an envelope and two slickers and three pairs of boots, one for her and two for Coco!

"Your outfits are charming, and we love your spunk and enthusiasm," Mrs. Delarosa said, shaking Lauren's hand and then Coco's tiny white paw. "Especially Coco's!"

"Thank you very much!" Lauren said as moths and monarchs zoomed through her stomach. She and Coco posed for a formal photo that would appear in the newspaper.

Well . . . not too formal. Lauren's dress was wrinkled, her wreath was crooked, and Coco's sweater was unraveling.

"Cheese!" Lauren said as the flash went off.

"*Yip!*" barked Coco.

Who cared what they looked like? They had won!

"These are so good," Lauren said, daintily munching a butterfly fry. Even though it looked like butterfly wings, it was really just a potato sliced in a special way and then fried.

"I like mine with lots and lots of ketchup," Emily said, squirting more on hers. After Lauren had collected her prizes and posed for photos, her parents had set her and her friends up at a picnic table with plates of fries and cups of apple cider before going back to get some coffee.

"Your trophy is so nice," Sam said, touching the gold-colored maple leaf prize. Lauren had put it in the middle of the table.

"And when you get your name engraved on

it, it will be even nicer," Kaia said, swallowing some cider.

Coco had been sitting in Lauren's lap. Now she stood up on her toes and, without warning, stole a fry from Emily's plate.

"Yuck!" Lauren exclaimed. Coco was covered from head to furry white paw with ketchup! "How am I going to get you clean?"

"That's easy," Emily said. She reached over and dipped her fry in Coco's fur, then popped it in her mouth. "Yum-meee!"

"Ewww!" Lauren cried. Then Kaia giggled. And so did Sam. And then so did Lauren. Pretty soon they were all laughing like crazy—and gobbling up fries.

"You guys can be pretty silly, can't you?" Sam asked, still giggling. She had ketchup on her nose.

"It's one of the requirements of the Woof! Club," Emily told her.

Lauren loved being silly sometimes. She'd

have plenty of time to be grown up. "Just like you will too," she said to Coco, squeezing her tight. Today hadn't gone as she'd expected . . . but she'd had a ton of fun.

"I'm *glad* you're still a puppy," she said as Coco grabbed another fry, this time from Kaia. "Who knows how many surprises you have waiting for me?"

DOG TIPS

HOW TO FEED YOUR DOG AND KEEP HER HEALTHY!

Nothing is more important than making sure your dog has the right food. A healthy diet will give your dog the energy she needs and keep her body working properly. Just like you, a dog needs carbohydrates, fats, proteins, vitamins, and minerals. However, it's important to remember that what is healthy for a person may not be healthy for a dog. Dogs require different nutrients—and in different proportions—than people do. Pet food companies create food for pets that is nutritionally balanced and tastes good.

It may be tempting to feed your dog the food you like. But once you give a dog table scraps, it can be hard to stop. Table scraps alone aren't enough to keep your dog healthy, and they can contribute to weight problems. Some families don't give their dogs any people food. Some families make exceptions.

The important thing is to make sure your dog has the food she needs to be happy and healthy.

Dog Bowls

Make sure your dog knows where she can find her water and food bowls. Remember that bowls are for holding food—they aren't toys. If you have more than one dog, make sure each dog has her own bowl. You wouldn't want to eat from someone else's dish, would you? And when dogs eat from the same a bowl, it's hard to be sure each dog is getting her fair share.

A dog should always have access to fresh water. Keep the bowl full—and don't forget to clean it! You can get a bowl that's designed to be "no-spill" and is heavy enough that it won't move if a dog tries to push it—or carry it in her teeth!

What should you feed your dog?

Dog food is divided into three categories, each with differences in convenience, cost, taste, and nutritional value:

Dry: Simply pour it into the bowl and give it to your pet! You may need to moisten it with hot water.

You don't need to refrigerate dry food. This type of food has the highest energy content.

🍖 **Semi-moist:** You may need to mix this food with a carbohydrate before giving it to your dog. Follow the instructions on the label.

🍖 **Canned:** You may need an adult's help to open the can. Make sure to refrigerate what you don't use, and remember to use the leftover food within twenty-four hours. Canned foods contain a lot of water and don't provide as much energy as other foods. Large dogs will need to eat large amounts.

You can buy food for your dog at grocery and discount stores, as well as at specialty feed and pet stores. Your veterinarian is the best source of information. He can tell you what kind of food is best for your dog.

Your veterinarian may put your dog on a special diet. This may be permanent, or it may be temporary, to help a sick dog feel better.

When should you feed your dog?
And how much should you feed her?

Some pet owners have food available for their dogs at all times. Others keep their dogs on a strict feeding schedule. Again, these choices depend on your family—your schedule, the dog food you choose, and your dog's age and health. Your veterinarian can help you determine the right amount of food for your dog. Your dog food will also have instructions on the label to guide you.

What else do dogs like to eat?

Bones! But bones can cause choking, especially small bones that can lodge in a dog's mouth or throat. Never give your dog small bones. Check with your veterinarian to see what she says about other types of bones.

Chews! These are usually a safe substitute for bones.

Biscuit treats!

Never let your dog eat chocolate. Chocolate is toxic to pets.

Doggie Diets

Different dogs have different dietary needs. All of these dogs require special diets:

- Puppies
- Very active dogs
- Older dogs
- Pregnant dogs
- Overweight dogs
- Dogs with health problems

A Dalmatian puppy eats differently from a two-year-old Dalmatian. A pregnant dog needs enough nutrients to produce healthy puppies. A dog with kidney disease may benefit from a low-protein diet. A large, powerful dog such as a bullmastiff eats more than a dachshund. Some dogs need a few hundred calories a day—and some need a few thousand!

A dog can't feed herself—she relies on you and your family to give her food that tastes good and is good for her. Feeding your dog a nutritious diet is one of the most important—and loving—things you can do for your dog!

About the Author

Although she does not presently have a dog, Wendy Loggia has always loved them. Growing up, she was the proud owner of Rebel, a Siberian husky–German shepherd mix; Muffins, a toy poodle; and Nuisance, an adorable mutt who was part of her family for fifteen years. She's looking forward to the day when a furry-legged friend curls up at her feet again!

Official Rules & Regulations

I. HOW TO ENTER

NO PURCHASE NECESSARY. Enter by printing your name, your parent's name, your dog's name, your address and phone number, your date of birth, and a paragraph (250 words or less) stating why your dog is the picture-perfect pooch on a 3" x 5" index card. Attach a photo of your dog and mail to: Picture-Perfect Pooch Contest, Random House Marketing Department, 19th Floor, New York, NY 10036. Contest ends May 30, 2001, and all entries must be received no later than 5:00 p.m. Eastern Time on that date. LIMIT ONE ENTRY PER PERSON. Entries (including photographs) will not be returned.

II. ELIGIBILITY

Contest is open to residents of the United States, excluding Puerto Rico and the state of Florida, who are between the ages of 7 and 10 as of May 30, 2001. All federal, state, and local regulations apply. Void wherever prohibited or restricted by law. Employees of Random House, Inc., its parents, subsidiaries, and affiliates, their immediate family members, and persons living in their household are not eligible to enter this contest. Random House, Inc., is not responsible for postage due, lost, stolen, illegible, incomplete, or misdirected entries.

III. PRIZES

Grand Prize

One winner will have his/her dog's likeness, name, or photo appear in an upcoming Woof! book to be determined by Random House Children's Books.

Second Prize

Ten runner-ups will each receive a Picture-Perfect Pooch dog tag for their dog's collar.

Third Prize

One-hundred entries will receive a Picture-Perfect Pooch paper picture frame.

Approximate retail value of total prizes is $500 U.S.

IV. WINNER

Winners will be chosen on or about June 15, 2001, from all eligible entries received within the entry deadline by the Random House Marketing Department. Entries will be judged by Random House Marketing Department staff on the basis of originality, style, and creativity; decisions of the judges are final. The prize will be awarded in the name of the winner's parent or legal guardian. Random House will not be able to return your entry; please keep a copy for your records. Winners will be notified by mail on or about June 30, 2001; no other entrants will be notified. Taxes, if any, are the winner's sole responsibility. RANDOM HOUSE RESERVES THE RIGHT TO SUBSTITUTE PRIZES OF EQUAL VALUE IF PRIZES, AS STATED ABOVE, BECOME UNAVAILABLE. Winner's parent or legal guardian will be required to execute and return, within 14 days of notification, affidavits of eligibility and release. A noncompliance within that time period or the return of any notification as undeliverable will result in disqualification and the selection of an alternate winner. In the event of any other noncompliance with rules and conditions, prize may be awarded to an alternate winner.

V. RESERVATIONS

Entering the contest constitutes consent to the use of each winner's name, likeness, and biographical data (and the use of the name and likeness of each winner's pooch) for publicity and promotional purposes on behalf of Random House with no additional compensation or further permission (except where prohibited by law). Other entry names will NOT be used for subsequent mail solicitation. For the names of the winners, available after June 30, 2001, please send a stamped, self-addressed envelope to: Random House, Picture-Perfect Pooch Winners, 1540 Broadway, 19th Floor, New York, NY 10036.

Make Your Dog Famous!

Win a chance for your dog to be included in an upcoming Woof! book.

Think your dog is the cutest canine ever?
Then enter your mutt's mug in our contest and, if you win, your dog's picture will appear in an upcoming Woof! book! Second and Third prizes are also available. To enter, write a paragraph explaining why *your* dog is the picture-perfect pooch! Attach a photo of your dog and send it to:

Picture-Perfect Pooch Contest
Random House Marketing Dept.
1540 Broadway, 19th Floor,
New York, NY 10036.

See **official contest rules**
on the next page or visit
our Web site at
www.randomhouse.com/kids